Thum

Written by Liz Miles

Illustrated by Mel Armstrong

Collins

Fran cracks eggs for lunch.

The shell splits. A thing jumps into the sink.

3

Fran claps.

Thumper gets bigger. Her tail gets stronger.

Thumper chomps the food and drinks
the milk.

She bumps into a lamp and snaps
a chair.

A thrash from her tail cracks
the desk.

In the end, Mum shoos Thumper into the yard.

Thumper is glad. She helps cut the crops.

Fran helps pick the plums.

Then Fran brings Thumper her lunch.

crunch
crunch

Thumper naps in a tent next to the pond.

Fran and Thumper

After reading

Letters and Sounds: Phase 4

Word count: 100

Focus on adjacent consonants with short vowel phonemes, e.g. *drink*.

Common exception words: the, into, she, we, to

Curriculum links (EYFS): Understanding the world

Curriculum links (National Curriculum, Year 1): Science: Animals, including humans

Early learning goals: Reading: read and understand simple sentences; use phonic knowledge to decode regular words and read them aloud accurately; read some common irregular words; demonstrate understanding when talking with others about what they have read

National Curriculum learning objectives: Reading/word reading: read accurately by blending sounds in unfamiliar words containing GPCs that have been taught; Reading/comprehension: understand both the books they can already read accurately and fluently and those they listen to by checking that the text makes sense to them as they read, and correcting inaccurate reading; making inferences on the basis of what is being said and done

Developing fluency

- Your child may enjoy hearing you read the book.
- Take turns to read a page. Discuss what voices you will use for Mum and Fran. Check your child responds to the punctuation, pausing for the ellipsis, commas and full stops, and emphasising the sentences that end in exclamation marks.

Phonic practice

- Turn to pages 6 and 7 and focus on the words with adjacent consonants. Model sound talking the word **chomps** (ch-o-m-p-s). Encourage your child to sound talk the following with you:

    drinks   milk   bumps   lamp   snaps

- Challenge your child to find and read words with adjacent consonants on other pages.

Extending vocabulary

- Discuss the meaning of verbs in the context of the story. Can your child think of a word or phrase with a similar meaning (synonym) to the following?

    page 3 **splits** (*breaks, halves*)   page 6 **chomps** (*chews, eats*)   page 8 **thrash** (*hit, swish*)